THE ROOTS OF VIOLENCE

GLORIA FOSTER

GLOBAL
PUBLISHING
SOLUTIONS

THE ROOTS OF VIOLENCE by Gloria Foster

Published by Global Publishing Solutions, LLC
923 Fieldside Drive
Matteson, Illinois 60443
www.globalpublishingsolutions.com

Cover Design by Rebecacovers

Library of Congress Control Number:
2023941354
International Standard Book Number:
979-8-9886045-2-5
E-book International Standard Book Number:
979-8-9886045-3-2

Printed in the United States of America

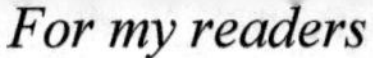

For my readers

THE ROOTS OF VIOLENCE

In shadows deep, where darkness thrives, a tale of violence, our world contrives. Roots entwined in hearts, unseen, a cycle of pain, a relentless machine.

From streets unrest, where anger reigns, the seeds are sown, in hearts and veins. A wounded soul, aching to be heard, lashing out, with every bitter word.

But beneath the surface, a truth awaits, a flicker of hope, against cruel fates. For in understanding, lies a potent key, to break the chains, set humanity free.

With empathy's embrace, we'll seek the light, to heal the wounds, and make things right. Unearth the causes, address the strife, and cultivate love to transform this life.

In the depths of despair, where shadows grow, a journey begins, for love to bestow. Roots of violence entangled deep within, a quest for healing, where compassion will win.

From troubled streets, where rage takes hold, seeds of discord planted, stories untold. Yearning for solace, voices cry to be heard, seeking understanding, with each uttered word.

Beneath the surface, a glimmer of grace, a path to redemption, in every embrace. Unlocking the secrets, a powerful key, breaking the cycle, setting humanity free.

With empathy's touch, we'll ignite the flame, mending the wounds, bringing peace without shame. Addressing the causes, forging a new way, love as the catalyst, for brighter days.

In this journey we embark, together we'll stride, transforming the darkness, with hope as our guide. The roots of violence, we'll unweave and unlace, building a world where harmony finds its place.

Gloria Foster

TABLE OF CONTENTS

INTRODUCTION

In a world where beauty and darkness coexist, this book unveils narratives that delve deep into the human experience, exploring resilience, hope, and the relentless pursuit of a brighter tomorrow. It is a collection of stories that boldly confront adversity, inner-city violence, and systemic injustice.

Within these pages, you will meet individuals who, despite their surroundings, rise above the challenges they face. Their journeys reflect the indomitable human spirit, driven by determination and an unyielding belief in the potential for change.

Through the voices of Mary, Sheila, Jonathan, Xavier, and Tobias, among others, we will share in their triumphs, heartaches, and moments of enlightenment. Their stories are not solitary; they are threads woven into a broader narrative, representing the collective journey towards a more just and equitable society.

Themes of community, education, justice, healing, and reconciliation resound throughout these stories. They underscore the characters' growth as they discover their voice, confront their fears, and navigate the complexities of their world. These stories remind us that while change starts with an individual, true transformation necessitates collective effort and solidarity.

As we embark on this journey, we admire the courage and resilience of those who have shared their stories. We acknowledge their experiences, both uplifting and challenging, and we reflect on the systems and structures that perpetuate violence and inequality. Let these stories inspire us to take action, both in our lives and within our communities.

This book invites us to explore the potent force of storytelling, challenging our perspectives, sparking empathy.

A GLIMPSE INTO THE PAST

As Jonathan leaned back in his chair, his gaze fixed on the old oak tree that had stood proudly in the front yard of their childhood home. The warm breeze rustled the leaves, evoking memories of a time when life was simpler and he and his brother, David, were inseparable.

Growing up in a close-knit family, Jonathan and David were blessed with loving and supportive parents. Their father, a wise and gentle man, had instilled in them the importance of integrity and standing up for what is right. Their mother, a beacon of warmth and compassion, had nurtured their spirits, encouraging them to chase their dreams.

As Jonathan reminisced, his mind drifted to a vivid recollection of a summer evening spent on that very porch. The fading sunlight painted a golden hue across the sky, casting a warm glow on their faces. David sat next to him, his eyes shining with mischief and curiosity.

"Do you ever wonder what lies beyond these hills, Jon?" David's voice held a mixture of excitement and contemplation.

As Jonathan chuckled, his gaze fixed on the distant horizon. "All the time, little brother. I often imagine a world filled with endless adventures and boundless possibilities."

David grinned, his eyes sparkling with excitement. "Really, Jon? Like what?"

"Oh, you know," Jonathan replied, his voice filled with enthusiasm. "Exploring uncharted lands, sailing on pirate ships, flying to far-off galaxies, and maybe even discovering hidden treasures."

David's eyes widened, captivated by his older brother's vivid imagination. "Wow, that sounds amazing! I wish we could do all of that."

"We can, in our minds," Jonathan said, a playful glint in his eyes. "Our imagination can take us anywhere we want to go, little bro. We just have to believe in the magic of our dreams."

David nodded, his young heart eager to embrace the idea. "I believe, Jon. I believe in all of it."

"Good," Jonathan said, ruffling his brother's hair affectionately. "Because as long as we have each other, there's no adventure we can't embark on together."

Their conversation continued late into the night as they shared dreams and aspirations. They talked about their hopes of making a difference, of creating a world where justice and compassion prevailed. Their words were infused with youthful idealism, painting a vision of a future they both longed to see.

Their parents, sitting nearby, listened intently to their sons' conversation. Their eyes filled with pride, seeing the bond and ambition shared between Jonathan and David. They had always believed in their sons, nurturing their dreams and supporting their endeavors.

In that moment, the porch became a sanctuary of love and possibility. Time stood still as the family basked in the warmth of their connection, knowing that these cherished moments would shape the course of their lives.

As the years went by, life would test their resolve, challenging them in unexpected ways. But the memory of that porch conversation remained etched in Jonathan's heart, reminding him of the dreams they had once shared.

Silence settled between them, but their unspoken bond spoke volumes. Jonathan looked at David, recognizing the journey they had traveled together. Through the highs and lows, their brotherhood had remained steadfast, an unwavering source of strength.

Their parents, sensing the weight of their conversation, joined them on the porch. The four of them sat together, enveloped by a sense of love and support that only a family could provide. They exchanged stories, laughter, and tears, finding solace in each other's presence.

As the evening drew to a close, Jonathan looked up at the old oak tree, its branches stretching toward the sky. It stood as a silent witness to their journey, a symbol of strength and resilience.

With a renewed sense of purpose, Jonathan vowed to honor the dreams they had woven on that porch. He would carry their shared vision into the world, embracing the values their parents had instilled in them. Together, they would strive to create a better tomorrow, where justice and compassion reigned supreme.

As the first chapter of their lives unfolded, the echoes of their childhood conversations lingered in the air, reminding them of the unbreakable spirit that bound them together. They were ready to face the challenges ahead, drawing strength from their shared memories and the unwavering support of their family.

The journey to make a difference had just begun, and Jonathan stood determined, carrying the torch of their dreams. The roots of violence would be unearthed, and in their place, seeds of love and understanding would grow, shaping a future that mirrored the hopes they held dear.

With the love of family and the courage of their convictions, Jonathan and David stepped forward, ready to embark on a path that would forever change their lives and the lives of those around them.

THE UNFORGIVING NIGHT

In the heart of the neighborhood, under the cloak of darkness, a chilling event unfolded that would send shock waves through the community for years to come. It was a night of shattered tranquility when innocence collided with the harsh realities of life.

As the moon cast an eerie glow, a series of sharp screams shattered the silence, piercing through the stillness of the night. Panic and confusion rippled through the streets, as neighbors emerged from their homes, drawn by the anguished cries.

A young woman stood at the center of the chaos, her face etched with fear and desperation. Her pleas for help echoed through the night, reaching the ears of those who dared to venture outside. The air crackled with tension as the scene unfolded, attracting the attention of passersby who became witnesses to a crime that would forever haunt their memories.

Word spread like wildfire, and soon the police arrived with a sense of urgency, their flashing lights illuminating the darkness. They swarmed the area, trying to restore order and make sense of the chaos that had enveloped the neighborhood.

The night bore witness to a tragedy, an event that cast a long shadow over the community. Speculation filled the air, and whispered rumors spread like wildfire, painting an intricate web of theories and suspicions. The truth remained elusive, concealed within the veil of uncertainty that shrouded the incident.

In the aftermath of that unforgiving night, the lives of those directly involved would be forever altered. The event had unleashed a storm of emotions and consequences that would ripple through the community, leaving an indelible mark on the hearts and minds of those who bore witness.

SHADOWS OF DECEPTION

The night was thick with tension as David found himself ensnared in the cruel clutches of a plot designed to condemn him. The events that would forever change his life began with an ordinary evening, unsuspecting of the storm that loomed on the horizon.

As the clock ticked past midnight, a knock at David's door shattered the tranquil silence. Startled, he cautiously opened the door, only to be met with a group of stern-faced police officers, their eyes hardened by a hidden agenda. Without a word, they forcefully entered his home, their presence suffocating the once-familiar air.

Confusion and fear gripped David's heart as he was handcuffed, his protests falling on deaf ears. He was led outside, his neighbors watching with hushed whispers, their curiosity mingling with a growing sense of unease. The darkness of the night seemed to mirror the shadow cast upon David's life as he was escorted to the waiting police car, the cold metal of the seat matching the chill in his bones.

Inside the confines of the vehicle, David's mind raced, desperately searching for an explanation. He knew deep within his being that he was innocent, but the weight of the accusations pressed upon him like an anchor dragging him down. As the patrol car made its way through the city streets, David's thoughts turned to his brother, Jonathan, his steadfast confidant and pillar of support.

With a heavy heart, David was finally granted a phone call. He fumbled with the receiver, his trembling fingers finding solace in the familiarity of the numbers. Jonathan's voice, filled with concern and disbelief, resonated through the earpiece. The words spilled forth, each one a lifeline of hope amidst the storm.

"Jonathan," David's voice quivered with a mixture of emotions, "they've taken me. They say I... I'm being framed for murder."

Silence hung in the air, a palpable weight pressing upon their connection. Jonathan's mind reeled, struggling to process the devastating news. The bond between the brothers tightened, their unspoken promise of unwavering support bridging the distance that separated them.

"I won't let them destroy you, David." Jonathan's voice brimmed with determination. "We will fight this together. I'll gather the best legal team, leave no stone unturned, and expose the truth. You are not alone in this."

As David's call ended, the steel bars of the jail cell closed in around him, an emblem of the injustice that had consumed his life. Yet, in that moment of despair, a flicker of hope ignited within him, fueled by the unwavering faith in his brother's unwavering dedication.

MANIPULATION UNVEILED

The Interrogation

Within the sterile confines of the interrogation room, David sat on the cold, metal chair, his heart pounding with a mix of fear and confusion. The air hung heavy with tension, as the two police officers, Detectives Reed and Anderson, flanked him with their stern gazes. Beads of sweat trickled down David's forehead, his hands clammy and trembling.

Detective Reed leaned forward, his voice laced with an air of authority. "David, we have evidence that implicates you in the murder of Sarah Miller. We know you were at the scene of the crime. It's in your best interest to confess."

Confusion clouded David's mind as he vehemently denied any involvement. "I didn't do it! I have no idea how my fingerprints ended up there. You're making a mistake!"

Detective Anderson leaned in, his eyes piercing. "Don't lie to us, David. We've got witnesses who saw you near the crime scene that night. Your alibi doesn't hold up."

The relentless barrage of accusations and false evidence weighed heavily on David's spirit. The officers twisted his words, exploiting his vulnerabilities, and manipulating the truth. With each passing moment, David's resolve wavered, a seed of doubt planted deep within his psyche.

Manufactured Evidence

In a dimly lit room tucked away from prying eyes, Detectives Reed and Anderson huddled around a cluttered desk, meticulously piecing together a web of deceit. They sifted through a trove of fabricated evidence, a sinister tapestry designed to secure a conviction.

Detective Reed held up a bloodstained shirt, smirking with satisfaction. "This will link David directly to the crime scene. We'll make sure it's found in his apartment."

Detective Anderson nodded, his eyes gleaming with malice. "And let's not forget the planted fingerprints. We've got to make it ironclad. Once the jury sees this, they won't have any doubts about his guilt."

The officers methodically planned each step, their commitment to injustice fueling their actions. They forged witness statements, doctored photographs, and meticulously constructed an airtight case against an innocent man. In the shadows, their malevolent orchestration took shape, ensnaring David in a web of lies from which escape seemed impossible.

UNVEILING SHADOWS

Jonathan's car idled, a sentinel amidst the urban decay of the neighborhood he had been exploring. This wasn't just another visit; it was a pilgrimage to unearth the shrouded truths that had claimed his brother's life. His relentless pursuit of justice and unwavering commitment to his brother's memory fueled his every step.

Clutched in his hand was a notebook filled with scribbled clues and a name that had emerged as a beacon of hope in his quest for answers - Maya Walker, a renowned investigative journalist with a reputation for exposing corruption. In this moment, she represented the promise of unveiling the shadows that had cast a pall over his family.

Taking a deep breath, Jonathan stepped out of his car, his gaze fixed on the apartment building before him. For weeks, he had immersed himself in this neighborhood, painstakingly piecing together fragments of a puzzle that had haunted him for years. The pain of his brother's death in prison remained as raw as the day it had happened, fueling his relentless drive for truth and justice.

As he approached the building's entrance, he couldn't shake the weight of anticipation that hung in the air. He had reached out to Maya Walker, pouring out his brother's story in a desperate plea for help. The journalist had agreed to meet him here, in this place that held the key to unraveling a web of deceit.

The door creaked open, revealing a determined woman with a notepad in hand, her eyes focused and intense. "Jonathan?" Her voice carried a mix of curiosity and compassion.

He nodded, his voice steady. "Yes, that's me."

Maya extended her hand in greeting, her firm handshake mirroring her resolute demeanor. "I've read your brother's case file. It's a disturbing tale of corruption and injustice."

Jonathan's jaw clenched at the mention of the case file, the weight of it all crashing over him. "They took his life and framed him for a crime he didn't commit. But I won't rest until I've uncovered the truth and those responsible are held accountable."

Maya's gaze met his with unwavering intensity. "I'm here to help you do just that. Let's start by going over what you've uncovered so far."

In the days that followed, Jonathan and Maya delved into the labyrinth of deceit that had led to his brother's demise. They meticulously reviewed evidence, reexamined witness statements, and untangled a complex network of corrupt officers and guards. With each revelation, their resolve grew stronger, fueled by the shared determination to expose the truth.

During their investigation, Jonathan revisited the prison where his brother had spent his final days. Walking those halls, he felt a surge of emotions - anger, grief, and an unyielding sense of purpose. The memories of his visits to David flooded back, accompanied by the heaviness of knowing that his brother had suffered within these walls.

As he stepped back into the sunlight, Maya at his side, he voiced what had been haunting him. "David didn't deserve this. He deserved justice, a chance at redemption."

Maya's voice was soft but resolute. "And we're going to make sure he gets that justice, Jonathan."

Their collaboration bore fruit as they uncovered damning evidence of corruption within the prison. Conversations with former inmates and staff painted a chilling picture of abuse of power and a system that had failed David and countless others.

Jonathan's resolve never wavered, even as the investigation led them into dangerous territory. With Maya's guidance, he confronted his fears and the shadows that had lingered for so long. He forged ahead, despite threats and intimidation, driven by the need to honor his brother's memory and unveil the truth.

Months of relentless work culminated in a series of groundbreaking exposés authored by Maya. The articles laid bare the extent of corruption within the prison system and the lives it had shattered. The public outrage that followed was a testament to the power of their efforts.

In a courtroom, the corrupt officers and guards faced the consequences of their actions. Maya's investigative work had provided the foundation for a legal battle that had been years in the making. As the gavel fell, Jonathan felt a mixture of closure and the beginnings of healing.

Maya's presence at his side as the verdict was read served as a reminder that even in the face of darkness, justice could prevail. As they left the courtroom, Jonathan couldn't help but reflect on the journey that had led them here. His brother's memory had driven him to expose corruption, to challenge the status quo, and to ultimately bring about change.

As they walked out into the daylight, Jonathan felt a renewed sense of purpose. The shadows of the past had been illuminated, and he was determined to continue fighting for justice, not just for his brother, but for all those who had been wronged by a broken system. The path ahead was uncertain, but he knew that with Maya by his side, he had the strength to forge ahead, seeking truth and redemption.

A HEALING CONVERSATION

Jonathan stood outside the courthouse, his heart heavy with the weight of recent events. He had finally achieved justice for his brother, and the corrupt police officers responsible for the wrongful conviction were now behind bars. But amidst the closure, a sense of emptiness lingered, and he knew there was still much work to be done in his community.

As he reflected on the journey that had brought him here, he noticed a familiar face emerging from the courthouse doors. It was Detective Sarah Miller, the lead investigator who had relentlessly pursued the truth alongside him. Jonathan approached her, a mixture of gratitude and determination in his eyes.

"Detective Miller," Jonathan said, his voice filled with appreciation. "I couldn't have done this without your unwavering support and dedication."

Detective Miller nodded, her expression reflecting a sense of closure as well. "We did it, Jonathan," she replied. "Your determination to seek the truth and our collective efforts brought justice to your brother."

Jonathan agreed, but there was still one more conversation he needed to have. "There's someone else I need to talk to," he said, his tone resolute.

Detective Miller understood the unspoken words in Jonathan's eyes. "I can arrange that," she said, knowing that this conversation was a crucial step in the healing process.

A few days later, Jonathan found himself sitting across from Officer Markham, one of the corrupt police officers who had framed his brother. Markham's face bore the weight of guilt and remorse, and he looked up at Jonathan with a mix of shame and sorrow.

"I'm so sorry," Markham began, his voice trembling. "I was part of the injustice that your brother suffered. I followed orders without questioning, and I've regretted it every day since."

Jonathan listened, his anger giving way to empathy. He had walked a long road to justice, and now he saw an opportunity for redemption, not only for his brother but for Markham as well.

"I believe you," Jonathan said, his voice filled with forgiveness. "What's important is that you're here now, willing to make amends."

Markham nodded, tears in his eyes. "I want to help," he said. "I want to do whatever it takes to right this wrong."

Jonathan extended his hand, sealing a pact of redemption and healing. "Then let's work together," he said. "To ensure that no one else suffers the injustice my brother did."

As they shook hands, a sense of closure and a newfound determination filled the room. Jonathan knew that the road ahead was still challenging, but with the truth revealed and the commitment to positive change, he was ready to face whatever lay ahead, forging a path toward a more just and equitable community.

SHEILA'S DREAM

Sheila Leclaire tossed and turned in her bed, unable to shake off the feeling of dread that had crept into her mind. Her body was soaked in sweat, and her heart raced like a steam engine, threatening to burst out of her chest. She had just woken up from a dream that felt too real to be a mere figment of her imagination.

In the dream, she had found herself in a barren house, with an old, frail woman sitting in the corner. The woman looked like she was on the verge of death, and Sheila could hear the raspy sound of her labored breathing. What struck her the most was that the house had no walls, and she could see the dark, murky sky beyond.

Sheila tried to shake off the feeling of foreboding that had taken hold of her. It was just a dream, she told herself, trying to reason with the irrational fear that threatened to overwhelm her. But she knew that it was more than that. It was a premonition, a warning of something terrible that was about to happen.

She tried to recall every detail of the dream, hoping to make sense of it. But the more she tried to remember, the more elusive the memory became. All she could remember was the old woman's face, etched with wrinkles and lines, and the overwhelming feeling of dread that had washed over her.

She sat up in bed, the sheets twisted around her legs, and tried to calm her racing heart. She needed to clear her head and think rationally. She got out of bed, put on her robe, and went to the kitchen to make herself a cup of black tea. Maybe the warm drink would soothe her nerves and help her relax.

As she sipped her tea, she looked out the kitchen window, watching the first rays of sunlight peeking over the horizon. She knew she wouldn't be able to go back to sleep now, not with the dream still fresh in her mind. She decided to go for a walk, hoping that the fresh air would help her clear her head.

Sheila put on her sneakers, grabbed her phone, and headed out the door. She lived in a quiet, upscale neighborhood, where the streets were lined with manicured lawns and expensive cars. It was a far cry from the inner-city neighborhoods that were plagued by violence and crime.

As she walked, she tried to push the dream to the back of her mind, but it kept resurfacing, like a nagging itch that wouldn't go away. She knew she needed to talk to someone about it, but who? She couldn't confide in Jonathan, her trusted best friend, who was a lawyer known for his logical explanations. She didn't want to burden anyone close to her, as they all had their own challenges and responsibilities to handle.

Sheila walked for what felt like hours, lost in thought, until she found herself in front of an old, abandoned house. It was a stark contrast to the pristine houses she was used to seeing in her neighborhood. This house had peeling paint, broken windows, and overgrown weeds. It looked like it hadn't been inhabited for years.

But something about the house called out to her, as if it had a message to deliver. Sheila approached the house cautiously, her heart racing in her chest. As she got closer, she saw an old woman sitting on a chair in the front yard, staring blankly ahead.

Sheila approached the woman slowly, unsure of what to expect. "Excuse me, ma'am," she said softly. "Are you okay?"

The woman didn't respond. She just kept staring ahead, her eyes devoid of any emotion. Sheila realized that the woman was in a state of shock, and she wondered how long she had been sitting there. Sheila looked to see if anyone else was nearby, but the street was deserted. She knew she couldn't leave the woman there, alone and vulnerable. Sheila approached the woman and gently touched her shoulder. "Ma'am, can I help you? Do you need me to call someone for you?"

The woman looked at Sheila, her eyes filled with tears. "He's gone," she said, her voice barely above a whisper.

Sheila didn't know who the woman was talking about, but she could feel the woman's pain. "I'm so sorry," she said, placing a comforting hand on the woman's back.

The woman looked at Sheila, as if seeing her for the first time. "Who are you?" she asked, her voice trembling.

"My name is Sheila," she said. "I live in the neighborhood. Can I help you in any way?"

The woman shook her head. "No, no one can help me. He's gone forever."

Sheila didn't know what to say, but she felt a connection with the woman, a shared sense of loss. She sat down on the grass next to the woman and listened as she poured out her heart. The woman told her about her son, who had been killed in a car accident the night before. He was the light of her life, her reason for living, and now he was gone. Sheila listened, tears streaming down her face, and held the woman's hand.

After a while, the woman's sobs subsided, and she looked at Sheila with gratitude. "Thank you," she said. "You're an angel. I don't know what I would have done without you."

Sheila smiled, feeling a sense of peace and fulfillment. She knew that the dream she had had earlier that morning was a premonition, a warning that she needed to help someone in need. And she had listened to that call, even though it had taken her out of her comfort zone. As she walked back to her house, Sheila felt a sense of purpose and clarity. She knew that she had a gift, a sixth sense that allowed her to see beyond the surface of things. And she was determined to use that gift to help others, to make a difference in the world.

THE SHOOTING

Sheila sat in her spacious living room, watching the news coverage of the shooting that had taken place just blocks from her home. The reporters were speculating about the cause of the violence, but Sheila knew the truth: this was just the latest in a long line of incidents that had plagued her community.

She couldn't shake the feeling that her dream had been a warning of this event. The barren house with the frail woman sitting inside... it all felt like a premonition. Sheila knew she had to do something to stop the violence from continuing.

She called Jonathan and Valencia, her two closest friends, and asked them to meet her at her house. When they arrived, Sheila greeted them with a warm embrace.

"I can't believe this is happening," she said, her voice trembling. "I had a feeling that something like this was going to happen, but I didn't know it would be this bad."

Jonathan placed a reassuring hand on her shoulder. "We're here for you, Lady Love. Whatever you need, we've got your back."

Valencia nodded in agreement. "We need to figure out what's causing all of this violence and put a stop to it. We can't just sit back and watch our community fall apart."

The three friends spent the rest of the day brainstorming ideas for how to stop the violence. They talked to community leaders and law enforcement officials and even visited local schools to talk to the students about the dangers of violence.

But as the days went on, it became clear that their efforts weren't enough. The violence continued to escalate, and the community was on edge.

One day, Sheila received a phone call from Jonathan. "I need you to meet me at the bar," he said, his voice urgent. "We need to talk."

Sheila hurried to the bar, where she found Jonathan sitting at a table with Tobias and Xavier. The three men looked grave, and Sheila knew that something was amiss.

"What's going on?" she asked, taking a seat at the table.

Jonathan took a deep breath. "I've been working on a case... a murder case. And I think it might be connected to what's happening in our community."

Sheila's heart raced. "What do you mean?"

Jonathan explained that the murder victim was a young man from the inner city and that he had uncovered evidence that suggested the killer was connected to a larger network of criminal activity in the area.

"We need to take action," Xavier said, his voice firm. "We can't let this violence continue."

The four friends spent the rest of the night discussing their plan of action. They decided to launch their own investigation into the criminal network, working in secret to gather information and build a case.

As they worked, Sheila couldn't help but feel a sense of fear and unease. The violence in her community seemed to be getting worse by the day, and she knew that they were putting themselves in danger by taking on this mission.

But she also knew that she couldn't sit back and do nothing. She had to take a stand and fight for her community, no matter the cost.

JONATHAN'S CARJACKING

Jonathan's heart raced as he remembered the terrifying ordeal of being carjacked. He had been leaving work late one evening when he was ambushed by a group of young men. They had demanded his car, wallet, and phone. Jonathan had been in shock at first, but his legal training quickly kicked in, and he managed to stay calm and negotiate with his attackers.

As he recounted the incident to Sheila over the phone, he could hear the relief in her voice. She had been worried sick about him since she had her premonition. They talked for a while longer about the shooting and the murder case that Jonathan was working on. Sheila was intrigued and wanted to help in any way she could.

Jonathan filled her in on the details of the case. A young man named Devonte had been accused of killing a prominent businessman. The evidence against him was circumstantial, but the prosecutor was determined to secure a conviction. Jonathan had been hired by Devonte's family to represent him in court.

Sheila listened intently as Jonathan spoke. She knew firsthand how the justice system could fail people, especially those from inner-city communities. Her own father had been falsely accused of a crime and spent years in prison before being exonerated. Sheila had grown up seeing the inequalities of the system and was determined to make a difference.

As they ended the call, Sheila's mind raced with ideas. She knew that she had to do something to help Jonathan and Devonte. She couldn't sit idly by while another innocent person was railroaded by the system.

The next day, Sheila reached out to Valencia, Mary, and Allie. She knew that together they could make a difference. They met at a coffee shop in downtown Atlanta and discussed the recent violence and the case that Jonathan was working on.

Valencia was the first to speak up. "I teach math, but I also know statistics. The odds are stacked against our boys. Black men are more likely to be arrested and imprisoned than any other group. We have to fight for justice and equality."

Mary nodded in agreement. "My husband is a lawyer. He sees the same injustices every day. We need to use our resources and our voices to make a change."

Allie chimed in. "I own a marketing firm. We can use social media and other platforms to spread the word and raise awareness."

Sheila listened intently, feeling inspired by her friends' passion and determination. Together, they formed a plan to help Jonathan and Devonte.

Over the next few weeks, they held rallies, spoke at city council meetings, and reached out to the media. Their efforts paid off when a key witness came forward, revealing that they had seen someone else at the scene of the crime. The new evidence exonerated Devonte, and he was released from custody.

Jonathan was overjoyed when he heard the news. He had worked tirelessly on the case, and it was a victory for him and his team. But he knew that there was still much work to be done.

As he sat at the bar with Tobias and Xavier, he pondered the root causes of inner-city violence. "We need to address poverty, lack of education, and systemic racism. These are the issues that lead to crime and violence. We can't just lock people up and throw away the key. We have to invest in our communities and our people."

Tobias nodded in agreement. "We need more programs to provide job training, education, and mentorship. We need to break the cycle of poverty and give our young people hope for the future."

Xavier added, "And we need to address the trauma that so many of our young people have experienced. Violence begets violence. We need to provide counseling and support to help heal our communities and break the cycle of violence."

Jonathan and his friends began to put their ideas into action, starting with their own community. They reached out to local organizations, churches, and schools to form partnerships and create programs to address poverty, education, and trauma.

Allie's marketing firm helped to create a campaign that highlighted the successes of these programs, showing the positive impact that investing in communities could have. Valencia used her expertise in statistics to create reports and data analyses that could be presented to local officials to push for policy changes.

Mary and her husband worked on pro bono cases and advocacy work to address systemic issues within the justice system. Xavier used his connections in the mental health field to create support groups and counseling services for those affected by violence and trauma.

Their efforts slowly began to pay off, with increased funding for education and job training programs, changes in police policies and practices, and a shift toward restorative justice.

Jonathan continued to work as a lawyer, representing those who were falsely accused or wrongfully convicted, while also advocating for systemic change. He spoke at conferences and rallies, sharing his own experiences and calling for a more just society.

Over time, their efforts grew, spreading to other cities and states. They became a powerful force for change, inspiring others to take action and demand a better future for all.

As he looked back on his journey, Jonathan knew that it was the support of his friends that had helped him to find his purpose and make a difference. He was grateful for their passion and determination, and for the way they had come together to create a better world.

And as he looked ahead, he felt a sense of hope for the future. He knew that there were still challenges ahead, but he was confident that together, they could overcome them. For Jonathan and his friends, the fight for justice and equality was far from over, but they were ready to continue the journey, one step at a time.

THE MURDER CASE

Jonathan was determined to uncover the truth behind the murder case he had been assigned. Hours turned into days as he meticulously reviewed evidence, interviewed witnesses, and unraveled the intricate threads of the investigation. The deeper he delved, the clearer it became that this case was far from ordinary.

The web of deceit he uncovered extended far beyond the crime scene. Powerful figures in the community seemed to be pulling strings, manipulating justice to protect their interests. As Jonathan pieced together the puzzle, he knew he was treading dangerous waters. Threats came from unknown sources, but he refused to be intimidated. This was about more than just solving a case; it was about holding those responsible accountable and making the community safer.

Months of unwavering dedication led to a breakthrough, and justice was finally served. But Jonathan knew that arresting the criminals was just the beginning. He recognized that the roots of violence ran deep, intertwined with poverty, inequality, and lack of opportunities. He resolved to fight for lasting change, advocating for education, job opportunities, and support for at-risk youth.

With courage and conviction, Jonathan's efforts extended beyond the courtroom. He spoke at conferences, formed alliances, and challenged unfair policies. The impact of his work spread, touching lives far beyond his immediate community. Though the road ahead was challenging, he remained committed, knowing that every step towards justice mattered. Jonathan's journey was a testament to the power of perseverance as he continued to be a beacon of hope, inspiring a future where justice and equality prevailed.

A CONVERSATION AT THE BAR

The bar was dimly lit and filled with the sounds of chatter and glasses clinking together. Jonathan, Xavier, and Tobias sat at a corner table, nursing their drinks as they spoke.

"This violence, man. It's everywhere," Xavier said, shaking his head.

"I know," Jonathan replied. "It's like a disease that's infecting our communities. And it's not just about gangs and drugs. It's about poverty, lack of opportunities, and systemic racism."

Tobias nodded in agreement. "And the media only shows the sensational stories. They don't talk about the root causes or the people who are working to make a difference."

"Exactly," Jonathan said. "And that's why we need to keep digging and uncovering the truth. We can't just accept things as they are."

Xavier raised his glass. "To uncovering the truth, then."

They clinked their glasses together and took a sip of their drinks.

"So, Jonathan, what have you found out about the murder case?" Tobias asked.

Jonathan leaned forward, his voice low. "It's a mess. The victim was a young woman, a college student. She was shot in her apartment, and the evidence points to a police officer who was supposed to be investigating a drug case in the same building."

Xavier whistled. "That's heavy. Do you have any leads?"

"I have a few. But the problem is, the officer has powerful connections. It's like he's above the law."

Tobias nodded. "That's how it always is. The people with power and money can get away with anything."

"But we won't let them get away with this," Jonathan said firmly.

They continued talking late into the night, discussing the ways they could work together to make a difference in their communities. They talked about the importance of education, mentorship, and creating opportunities for young people.

As they left the bar, Xavier clapped Jonathan on the back. "Keep fighting the good fight, brother."

Jonathan smiled. "I will. And I know you will too."

As they went their separate ways, each man felt a renewed sense of purpose. They knew that the road ahead would be difficult, but they were committed to making a difference, one step at a time.

The next day, Jonathan woke up early, fueled by determination and a sense of urgency. He reached out to his network of contacts, setting up meetings with witnesses, gathering additional evidence, and following up on any leads that could shed light on the murder case. He also reached out to local community leaders, sharing his findings and seeking their support in advocating for justice. Together, they strategized ways to raise awareness and put pressure on the authorities to conduct a fair investigation.

Meanwhile, Xavier and Tobias used their respective skills and connections to rally support. Xavier, with his charismatic personality, organized community meetings, where people shared their stories and experiences of injustice. Tobias, on the other hand, used his tech-savvy nature to launch a social media campaign, spreading the word and garnering public attention. Their efforts began to gain traction. News outlets picked up the story, and public pressure intensified. The community started demanding accountability and a thorough investigation into the murder case.

Jonathan, Xavier, and Tobias became the faces of the movement, speaking at rallies, town hall meetings, and media interviews. They articulated the need for systemic change, highlighting how the murder case was emblematic of larger issues plaguing the community. Their relentless pursuit of truth and justice had a profound impact. People from all walks of life joined the cause, standing in solidarity with the victims and their families. The movement grew stronger, and the pressure on the authorities mounted.

As the investigation progressed, new evidence came to light, exposing a web of corruption and cover-ups within the police department. The officer suspected of the crime was eventually arrested, and the case was assigned to an independent prosecutor to ensure a fair trial. The trial became a pivotal moment for the community. It was a chance to confront the systemic issues that allowed such crimes to occur. The courtroom was filled with supporters, their presence a testament to the power of collective action. Jonathan, armed with his unwavering dedication, presented a compelling case, meticulously laying out the evidence and dismantling the defense's arguments. Witnesses came forward, their testimonies bolstering the prosecution's case against the corrupt officer.

Finally, after weeks of trial, the verdict was delivered. The officer was found guilty of murder and other charges, the jury recognizing the weight of his actions and the need for accountability. The community erupted in a mix of emotions—relief, vindication, and a renewed sense of hope. The victory was not just for the victim and her family but for everyone who had fought tirelessly for justice.

But Jonathan, Xavier, and Tobias knew that their work was far from done. They understood that this case was just one piece of a larger puzzle, and they were committed to addressing the underlying issues that perpetuated violence and corruption.

The friends continued their efforts, expanding their scope to advocate for police reform, community investment, and educational opportunities. They collaborated with lawmakers, pushing for legislative changes that would address systemic inequalities and prevent similar tragedies from happening again. The journey was arduous, and setbacks were inevitable. Yet, fueled by their shared vision and the support of the community, they pressed on. Their commitment to the cause became an inspiration, sparking a movement that spread far beyond their own community, igniting change in cities and towns across the country.

Jonathan, Xavier, and Tobias had started as three friends sitting in a dimly lit bar, but they had evolved into beacons of hope, catalysts for transformation, and tireless warriors for justice. With their collective efforts, they began to reshape their community, laying the foundation for a more equitable and safer future.

MARY'S PERSPECTIVE

Mary sat alone in her living room, deep in thought. The recent events had shaken her to her core, and she couldn't shake the feeling that something needed to change. She had grown up in a close-knit community in Sommerville, Virginia, where kindness and compassion were the pillars that held the neighborhood together.

As a wife and caring member of her community, Mary couldn't help but worry about the future. The rise of violence in nearby cities served as a stark reminder that no place was immune to the darkness that could infiltrate even the most idyllic settings. She knew that taking action was necessary to protect the lives of those she held dear and the place she called home.

Mary believed that addressing the root causes of violence required a collective effort. She envisioned a future where education, mentorship, and opportunities for growth would replace the allure of crime and despair. With determination in her heart, Mary set out to be a catalyst for change in her community, knowing that together, they could create a brighter, safer tomorrow. She picked up a pen and a notebook and began to write down her thoughts.

"I believe that the root causes of inner-city violence are complex and multifaceted. Poverty, lack of education, and systemic racism all play a role in perpetuating the cycle of violence that plagues our communities. But I also believe that there is hope for change.

"We must start by investing in our youth. Education is the key to breaking the cycle of poverty and providing a pathway to success. We need to provide resources and support to young people so that they can achieve their full potential. We must also address the issue of systemic racism and work to dismantle the structures that perpetuate inequality.

"But we cannot do this alone. It takes a collective effort to create real change. We need to work together as a community to address the root causes of violence and create a safe and healthy environment for all.

"I also believe that we need to change the narrative around violence. We need to stop glorifying violence in our media and our culture. We need to create positive role models and promote values such as empathy, compassion, and community.

"I know that change won't happen overnight, but I truly believe that if we work together and stay committed, we can create a brighter future for our communities and our families."

Mary set down her pen and reread her words. She felt a sense of hope and determination that she hadn't felt in a long time. She knew that it wouldn't be easy, but she was ready to take action and do her part to create a better world.

Mary's words resonated deep within her, igniting a fire within her soul. She knew that simply writing down her thoughts wasn't enough; action was necessary to bring about the change she envisioned. With a renewed sense of purpose, she embarked on her journey to make a difference.

Mary's first step was reaching out to like-minded individuals in her community. She organized meetings and gatherings, inviting neighbors, friends, and local leaders to discuss the issues and brainstorm solutions. Together, they formed a coalition committed to tackling the root causes of violence and creating a safer environment for all.

Education became a central focus of their efforts. Mary collaborated with educators, parents, and community organizations to develop programs that provided educational support and resources to underprivileged students. They advocated for increased funding for schools in low-income neighborhoods, pushing for equal opportunities for all children.

Recognizing the power of mentorship, Mary spearheaded a mentorship program where successful individuals from various professions volunteered their time to guide and inspire young people. The program not only provided guidance but also helped to broaden horizons and expose youth to different career paths and opportunities.

To address the systemic racism deeply ingrained in society, Mary worked with community leaders to advocate for policy changes and promote inclusivity. They pushed for fair hiring practices, equitable distribution of resources, and the dismantling of discriminatory practices that perpetuated inequality. Through awareness campaigns and allyship initiatives, they aimed to foster a more inclusive and accepting community.

Mary understood that changing the narrative surrounding violence required a multi-pronged approach. She collaborated with local artists, writers, and filmmakers to create and promote art that highlighted the stories of resilience, hope, and unity within their community. Through cultural events and exhibitions, they celebrated the rich diversity and the shared humanity that bound them together.

As Mary continued to take action, her efforts gained momentum. The community rallied behind her, recognizing the sincerity of her commitment and the positive impact they were making together. Local businesses offered their support, providing resources, funding, and mentorship opportunities for youth programs. Faith-based organizations joined the cause, advocating for peace, justice, and compassion in their sermons and community outreach.

Through perseverance and collective action, Mary and her community began to witness tangible changes.

Graduation rates improved, crime rates declined, and a newfound sense of unity and hope permeated the neighborhood. Their success became a beacon of inspiration for other communities grappling with similar challenges, sparking a ripple effect that spread far and wide.

Mary's living room, once a place of introspection, had transformed into a hub of activity and collaboration. The walls were adorned with posters, notes, and plans for community initiatives. Meetings and gatherings became a regular occurrence as the community became more engaged and empowered.

Years later, reflecting on the journey, Mary marveled at how a single act of writing down her thoughts had led to a powerful movement. The transformation of her community had been driven by the collective efforts and unwavering determination of individuals who refused to accept the status quo.

Mary's journey was far from over. She recognized that maintaining the progress they had achieved required continued dedication and vigilance. She knew that challenges would arise and setbacks were inevitable, but she remained steadfast in her belief that change was possible.

With her pen and notebook in hand, Mary looked toward the future, ready to face the obstacles and seize the opportunities that lay ahead. She knew that her community's transformation was an ongoing process, and she was committed to being an agent of change, creating a brighter and more hopeful future for generations to come.

SHEILA'S PLAN

Sheila's mind raced as she sat in her office, staring at the blank screen of her computer. The recent shooting in her community had left her feeling shaken and vulnerable, and she knew that something needed to be done to address the root causes of the violence.

As an investment banker, Sheila was used to tackling complex problems and coming up with innovative solutions. But this was different. This was personal. She couldn't stand by and watch as her community was torn apart by senseless violence.

Sheila reached for her phone and dialed Valencia's number. "Hey, Val, are you free for lunch today?" she asked.

"Sure, what's up?" Valencia replied.

"I want to talk to you about something," Sheila said cryptically.

"Okay, I'll meet you at that little cafe on Third Street at noon," Valencia said.

When Sheila arrived at the cafe, Valencia was already there, sipping on a cup of coffee. They hugged and exchanged pleasantries before getting down to business.

"What's going on, Sheila?" Valencia asked.

"I've been thinking a lot about the recent shooting," Sheila said. "I can't shake the feeling that something needs to be done to address the root causes of the violence."

Valencia nodded in agreement. "I've been feeling the same way. It's like we're just putting a Band-Aid on a gaping wound."

"Exactly," Sheila said. "And that's why I wanted to talk to you. I think we need to come up with a plan. Something comprehensive that addresses all of the issues that contribute to the violence in our community."

Valencia's eyes lit up. "I'm in. What do you have in mind?"

Sheila leaned forward, her eyes bright with enthusiasm. "Okay, so hear me out. I think we need to start by addressing the issue of poverty. We need to create more job opportunities and provide better access to education and training. That way, people have a way out of poverty and don't turn to violence as a means of survival."

Valencia nodded in agreement. "Yes, and we also need to address the issue of systemic racism. So many of our young people are growing up feeling hopeless and marginalized. We need to create a more equitable society where everyone has a fair shot at success."

Sheila smiled. "Exactly. And I think we can do that by creating partnerships between businesses and community organizations. We can provide mentorship, internships, and job training programs that help people build the skills and connections they need to succeed."

Valencia nodded. "That's a great idea. But we also need to address the issue of mental health. So many of our young people are dealing with trauma and don't have access to the resources they need to heal. We need to provide more counseling services and support for families who are dealing with these issues."

Sheila's smile faltered slightly. "That's a good point. But how do we pay for all of this? We can't expect the government to foot the bill."

Valencia leaned back in her chair, thinking. "I think we can start by reaching out to local businesses and community organizations. We can make the case that investing in the community is good for business, and we can offer them tax incentives and other benefits to get them on board."

Sheila nodded slowly. "Okay, that's a good start. But I think we also need to think bigger. We need to create a movement. Something that inspires people to get involved and take action."

Valencia's eyes widened. "I like where this is going. But how do we do that?"

Sheila leaned forward again, her eyes blazing with passion. "We need to create a campaign. Something that captures people's imaginations and inspires them to take action. We need to show that we are not just talking about change, but that we are actively working toward it. We need to involve everyone in our community, from the elders to the youth, and create a sense of unity and purpose. We need to take back our streets and make them safe for everyone. And we can do it, if we work together." Valencia nodded in agreement, and she raised her glass of iced tea. "To unity and purpose," she said. "To making a real difference in our community." Sheila and Valencia clinked their glasses together and drank, energized by the shared vision of a better future.

Agents of Change: Sheila and Valencia

Sheila and Valencia continued their lunch meeting, fueled by a shared determination to make a difference in their community. They brainstormed strategies and mapped out a comprehensive plan to address the root causes of violence.

Their first step was to gather data and research from local organizations, community leaders, and academic institutions. They wanted to understand the specific challenges their community faced and identify the most effective interventions. Sheila used her connections in the business world to secure funding for the research and program implementation.

Armed with knowledge, Sheila and Valencia mobilized a diverse team of volunteers passionate about creating change. They organized community forums and town hall meetings to engage residents and gather their input. They wanted to ensure that the solutions they proposed were community-driven and responsive to the unique needs and aspirations of the people they aimed to serve.

Recognizing the importance of collaboration, Sheila and Valencia reached out to local government officials, law enforcement agencies, and social service providers. They believed that a multi-sector approach was crucial to address the complex interplay of factors that contributed to violence. Together, they formed a task force dedicated to implementing the strategies outlined in their plan.

Education and economic empowerment emerged as key pillars of their strategy. They worked with schools and universities to expand educational opportunities, focusing on early intervention programs, after-school activities, and mentorship initiatives. They also engaged local businesses to create job training programs and apprenticeships, empowering individuals with marketable skills and pathways to employment.

To tackle systemic racism, Sheila and Valencia spearheaded diversity and inclusion training programs for businesses and organizations. They advocated for policies that promoted equal opportunities and worked to create safe spaces where open dialogue about race and equity could flourish.

In parallel, they partnered with healthcare providers and community organizations to increase access to mental health services. They established counseling centers and support groups, destigmatizing seeking help for trauma and providing the necessary resources for healing and growth.

As their efforts gained momentum, Sheila and Valencia knew they needed to raise awareness and build public support. They launched a media campaign, leveraging social media, local newspapers, and television stations to share stories of hope, resilience, and the transformative power of community-driven initiatives. They showcased the success stories of individuals who had overcome adversity and the positive impact their programs were having on reducing violence.

The movement grew, attracting volunteers, philanthropists, and influencers who recognized the importance of their cause. Sheila and Valencia organized community events, concerts, and art exhibitions that celebrated the vibrant culture and diversity of their community. These events provided opportunities for people to connect, share their stories, and join forces to bring about lasting change.

Over time, Sheila and Valencia's comprehensive approach began to yield tangible results. Graduation rates improved, crime rates decreased, and opportunities for economic advancement expanded. The once-vulnerable neighborhoods transformed into vibrant, safe communities where families thrived and young people saw a future filled with possibilities.

Sitting in her office years later, Sheila reflected on the transformative journey she and Valencia had embarked upon. The once-blank screen before her now displayed a slideshow of photos capturing the milestones and triumphs of their movement. She knew there was still work to be done, but the progress they had made filled her with hope and renewed determination.

Sheila's office had become a hub of activity, filled with a dedicated team of individuals who shared her passion for creating a safer and more inclusive community. Their collective efforts were a testament to the power of individuals coming together to drive change.

As Sheila continued her work, she saw the ripple effects of their efforts spreading far beyond their initial goals. The success of their community-driven initiatives caught the attention of neighboring towns and cities, inspiring them to adopt similar strategies and create their own movements for change.

Sheila became a sought-after speaker, traveling across the country to share the lessons learned from their journey. She spoke at conferences and universities and even appeared on national television, using her platform to advocate for policy reforms and challenge societal norms that perpetuated violence and inequality.

Back in her community, Sheila's team expanded, attracting talented individuals from diverse backgrounds who shared a common vision. Together, they developed innovative programs that addressed emerging challenges, such as cyberbullying, mental health in schools, and the impact of technology on youth well-being.

Recognizing the importance of sustainability, Sheila and her team worked tirelessly to secure long-term funding for their initiatives. They formed partnerships with corporations, foundations, and government agencies, leveraging their combined resources to ensure the continuity and growth of their projects.

As the years went by, Sheila witnessed the transformation of not just her community, but also herself. The work had changed her perspective, deepened her empathy, and strengthened her commitment to social justice. She became a mentor to young leaders, guiding them in their own efforts to make a positive impact in their communities.

Through it all, Sheila remained humble, always reminding herself that true change was a collective effort. She celebrated every small victory, knowing that each one represented a life touched, a family uplifted, and a step closer to a more just and peaceful society.

In time, Sheila's work became a legacy, inspiring future generations to take up the mantle of community activism and continue the fight for a better world. Her story became a beacon of hope, a testament to the power of individuals who refuse to accept the status quo and work tirelessly to create a brighter future.

And as Sheila looked out over her community, now thriving with opportunities and marked by unity, she couldn't help but feel a sense of profound gratitude. The road had been challenging, and there were still obstacles to overcome, but she knew that their collective efforts had made a lasting difference.

Sheila's journey had taught her that even in the face of adversity, change was possible. It started with a simple realization, a spark of determination, and a commitment to action. And as she continued her work, she remained steadfast in her belief that every individual had the power to contribute to a more peaceful and equitable world—one community at a time.

A BEACON OF RESILIENCE

Amelia Martinez had always been a woman of action. Born and raised in the vibrant neighborhood of Eastside Heights, she had witnessed both the beauty and the challenges that life in the community had to offer. Her journey toward becoming a beacon of resilience was intertwined with the lives of her neighbors, including the characters we've come to know.

One balmy summer evening, as the golden hues of the sunset painted the streets, Amelia sat on her porch, deep in thought. She had just returned from work at a local community center, where she had spent the day listening to the stories of residents—stories that bore witness to the profound impact of violence.

The neighborhood had long grappled with crime and the far-reaching consequences it wrought. As a dedicated member of the community, Amelia couldn't help but be affected by these stories. She knew that something needed to change, and it had to start with the voices of those who lived these experiences.

Amelia lived just a few houses down from Mary, a retired schoolteacher who had dedicated her life to education and mentorship. Their connection was more than geographical; it was rooted in a shared vision of a brighter future for the neighborhood's youth.

Amelia decided to host a gathering at her home, a place where neighbors often congregated. She envisioned it as an opportunity for residents to share their personal stories, to unburden themselves of the weight they carried, and to ignite a dialogue about the toll of violence. With invitations extended and her porch illuminated by strings of twinkling lights, she prepared for the evening ahead.

As her guests arrived, the atmosphere was charged with a mix of anticipation and trepidation. Families, young and old, took their seats on the porch, the warm breeze carrying the scent of homemade empanadas. Amelia stood at the center, her voice steady but empathetic.

"We've all felt the impact of violence in our lives," she began, her gaze sweeping across the faces of her neighbors, including Mary. "Tonight, I want to hear your stories. I want us to understand how it has affected us and our community."

The stories began to flow, raw and unfiltered. Maria, a single mother, spoke about the sleepless nights she endured, worrying about her son's safety. Carlos, a high school student, shared his fear of walking to school every day, knowing that danger lurked around the corner. Elderly Mr. Ramirez recalled a time when he felt safe taking evening strolls but now remained confined to his home.

Amelia listened intently, nodding in understanding, and occasionally offering words of comfort. The porch became a sanctuary where the weight of their experiences could be shared openly.

Juan, a young man with a passion for art, spoke about how violence had stolen his brother's dreams. "My little brother had a talent for painting," he said, his voice tinged with sorrow. "But he's too afraid to go outside now. He's given up on his dreams."

Amelia's heart ached as she heard these personal narratives of pain, fear, and shattered dreams. She knew that these were not isolated stories but a reflection of the pervasive impact of violence on the community. Her resolve deepened.

As the evening continued, the dialogue shifted from sharing experiences to discussing solutions. Juan proposed a community mural project, a way to reclaim public spaces and inspire hope. Maria suggested a neighborhood watch program to improve safety. Carlos spoke about the importance of mentorship and guidance for young people.

The energy on Amelia's porch was palpable, a collective determination to forge a path forward. Residents pledged their support for these initiatives, knowing that change had to come from within.

In the weeks that followed, the community rallied behind these projects. The mural, a vibrant testament to resilience, now adorned a once-vacant wall. The neighborhood watch program provided a sense of security, and young people like Carlos found mentors who encouraged their dreams.

Amelia's porch gatherings became a regular occurrence, a space for residents to share their triumphs and setbacks, to celebrate the small victories, and to lean on one another in times of need. Their stories, once hidden in the shadows, now illuminated a path toward a brighter future.

Amelia knew that the road ahead would be long, and challenges would persist. Yet, as she stood on her porch, surrounded by her resilient community, she couldn't help but feel a profound sense of hope. The power to transform their lives and their neighborhood lay within each of them, their voices and their stories a testament to the strength of the human spirit in the face of adversity.

THE FUTURE

As the celebration continued, the friends sat around a bonfire, basking in the warm glow and sharing their thoughts on the future. The crackling of the fire seemed to echo the passion and determination in their voices.

Mary spoke up first, her voice filled with conviction. "I believe that if we continue to work together, tirelessly and unwaveringly, we can create a world where everyone, regardless of their background, has access to the resources and opportunities they need to thrive. We need to dismantle the barriers that hold people back and address the systemic issues that perpetuate inequality."

Sheila nodded in agreement, her eyes shining with determination. "Absolutely. Education plays a vital role in breaking down those barriers. We need to ensure that our young people, the next generation of leaders, have the tools, knowledge, and support they need to succeed. We must invest in education at every level and provide equal opportunities for all."

Jonathan chimed in, his voice firm. "And we cannot forget the importance of holding our leaders accountable. We need leaders who genuinely care about creating safe and equitable communities, who listen to the voices of the marginalized, and who take concrete action to address the root causes of violence and injustice. Our collective power and advocacy can drive the change we seek."

Xavier's voice resonated with passion. "Change starts with us. We must embody the values we advocate for. It is not enough to demand change from others; we must be the change we want to see in the world. Through our actions, our compassion, and our commitment, we can inspire others to join us on this journey."

Tobias sat quietly for a moment, contemplating the weight of his words, before speaking with sincerity. "While we fight for justice and equality, we must also remember the power of forgiveness and healing. The scars of violence run deep, and acknowledging the pain and trauma is essential. We need to create spaces for healing and reconciliation, fostering understanding and empathy as we work toward a more compassionate society."

The group fell into a thoughtful silence, their collective vision intertwining in the air. Finally, Sheila broke the silence, her voice resolute. "Whatever the future holds, whatever challenges lie ahead, I know that we can face them together. We have proven time and again that when we unite our voices and efforts, we can accomplish anything. We are stronger together."

The group shared a heartfelt moment of camaraderie, feeling the strength and bond they had formed through their shared mission. As the night wore on, they continued to discuss their hopes and dreams for the future. They envisioned a world where violence was a distant memory, where everyone had equal access to opportunities, and where communities were built on trust, empathy, and justice.

As the night drew to a close, the group embraced each other tightly, cherishing the connection they had forged. They knew that their journey was far from over, but they felt a renewed sense of purpose burning within them. They understood that the road ahead would be arduous and challenging, but they were resolute in their commitment to make a positive difference.

The next morning, with hearts full of determination, the group reluctantly parted ways, each returning to their own communities with a renewed sense of purpose. They carried with them the shared vision of a better world, their spirits ignited and their souls driven by the belief that together, they could overcome any obstacle.

The road ahead shimmered with possibility, beckoning them toward the transformative change they sought. They knew that challenges awaited them, but armed with their collective strength, resilience, and unwavering belief in the power of unity, they were ready to face whatever came their way.

Their journey continued, propelled by hope and fueled by the shared dream of creating a world where everyone could not only survive but thrive and flourish in a nurturing and inclusive environment.

They embarked on a relentless pursuit of justice, armed with their unwavering determination and a firm belief that their collective efforts could bring about tangible change. With each step they took, they engaged with community leaders, organized grassroots campaigns, and amplified the voices of those who had long been silenced.

Their advocacy extended beyond their local communities, reaching regional and national platforms. Through impassioned speeches, impactful storytelling, and strategic alliances, they sparked conversations that challenged existing systems and inspired others to join their cause.

As their movement gained momentum, they encountered setbacks and faced formidable opposition. Yet, they remained resilient, drawing strength from the unwavering support and solidarity of like-minded individuals who recognized the urgency of their mission.

Through extensive research and data analysis, they exposed the intricate web of systemic inequalities that perpetuated violence and hindered progress. Armed with irrefutable evidence, they engaged in dialogue with policymakers, pushing for comprehensive reforms that would dismantle oppressive structures and create a framework for lasting change.

Their efforts bore fruit as they witnessed incremental shifts in legislation, policies, and public perception. The fruits of their labor manifested in improved access to quality education, increased job opportunities, and a more equitable justice system that prioritized rehabilitation over retribution.

Communities that were once plagued by violence began to experience a transformative healing process. The scars of the past slowly faded as individuals found solace in support networks, mental health services, and community-led initiatives that fostered unity, empathy, and understanding.

As their work continued, their vision expanded. Their collective dream of a world where everyone could thrive and flourish evolved into a global movement for social justice and equality. They connected with activists from diverse backgrounds, cultures, and continents, forging alliances that transcended geographical boundaries.

Together, they championed the rights of marginalized communities nationwide, sparking a revolution that rippled across the country. Their impact reached far and wide, inspiring a new generation of change-makers and igniting a spark of hope in the hearts of those who yearned for a brighter, more compassionate future.

In their unwavering pursuit, they knew that their journey was far from over. But fueled by hope and fortified by their shared dream, they pressed on, spurred by the unwavering belief that through collective action, they could reshape the nation and create a future where every individual could truly thrive and flourish, regardless of their circumstances.

ABOUT THE AUTHOR

Gloria Foster is an accomplished author known for her captivating storytelling and ability to delve into the depths of human experiences. With a keen eye for detail and a passion for exploring the complexities of the human psyche, she weaves narratives that both entertain and provoke thought.

Her debut novel, *The Mind*, introduced readers to a cast of unforgettable characters, captivating them with its compelling storyline and thought-provoking themes. It was received with critical acclaim, earning a coveted 5-star review from Readers' Favorite, a testament to Gloria's skill in crafting engaging narratives.

Continuing the journey of her characters, Gloria's second novel, *The Core*, takes readers on an exhilarating ride, blending unexpected twists with a touch of magic. As part of "The Women's Soul" series, *The Core* expands the world established in its predecessor, introducing new characters and delving deeper into the rich tapestry of interconnected lives.

Gloria's writing has garnered recognition beyond literary circles. Her screenplay adaptation of *The Mind* was honored as a 2021 Screenplay Award Finalist in the prestigious Page Turner Awards, further solidifying her talent as a versatile storyteller.

With a diverse educational background, Gloria brings a unique perspective to her writing. She holds a Bachelor of Arts degree in Mathematical Sciences from the University of Illinois at Springfield, a testament to her analytical thinking and attention to detail. This multidimensional approach permeates her storytelling, infusing her work with a blend of intellectual depth and creative flair.

In addition to her literary pursuits, Gloria maintains an active online presence through her author website at www.gloriafoster.com. Through her website, readers can connect with her, explore her latest projects, and stay updated on future releases.

As an author, Gloria Foster's passion lies in crafting narratives that resonate with readers, exploring the human condition, and shedding light on the complexities of the world we inhabit. With each new work, she invites readers to embark on profound journeys of self-discovery and connection.

The Roots of Violence stands as a testament to Gloria's dedication to her craft, as she fearlessly tackles the intricate dynamics of violence and advocates for positive change in our society. Through her writing, she challenges readers to examine their own beliefs and become catalysts for a more compassionate and just world.

Gloria Foster is an author to watch, as her powerful storytelling continues to captivate readers and ignite conversations that transcend the pages of her books. With a commitment to authenticity and a talent for crafting engaging narratives, she has established herself as a rising star in the literary world.

Thanks for reading! If you loved the book and have a moment to spare, I would really appreciate a short review as this helps new readers find my books.